Adeline

I hope you enjoy Adeline!

Mary Ann Hayes

Adeline

Mary Ann Hayes

Tate Publishing & Enterprises

Published by Tate Publishing & Enterprises, LLC
127 E. Trade Center Terrace | Mustang, Oklahoma 73064 USA
1.888.361.9473 | www.tatepublishing.com

Tate Publishing is committed to excellence in the publishing industry. The company reflects the philosophy established by the founders, based on Psalm 68:11,
"The Lord gave the word and great was the company of those who published it."

Book design copyright © 2011 by Tate Publishing, LLC. All rights reserved.
Cover design by Blake Brasor
Interior design by Nathan Harmony
Photos by Tanya Izadora Photography

Published in the United States of America

ISBN: 978-1-61777-796-7
1. Fiction / General
2. Fiction / Christian / General
11.05.19

Dedication

To my mother, Jackie, for the spirit of adventure she instilled in us all.

Acknowledgements

Thanks first to Patrick, my husband and life partner of over thirty years. Without your love and support on every level, *Adeline* would never have come to fruition. Thank you for believing in me and encouraging me to follow my dreams.

Special thanks to the Hard-Nosed Zealots Writers Critique Group that I have been blessed to be a member of for the past five years. Your guidance and encouragement has been invaluable. I love and appreciate you all. Thank you, authors Gloria MacKay, Erika Madden, Margo Peterson, Lani Schonberg,

Mary Trimble, Peggy Wendel, and the late Juanita Wagoner. You are the anchor that holds me fast to the center of my writing world.

Thanks also to my daughters, Erin and Staci, for believing in and encouraging their mom. They not only stood firmly behind me, they pushed me forward when I needed it. And thank you Nick, my son, and Tanya, my daughter-in-law, for cheerfully donating hours of technical support and tutelage. Your patience and assistance has been invaluable.

Last but not least, I thank my parents, Chuck and Jackie, for a childhood filled with opportunities to immerse myself in the glories of Mother Earth. It is a firefly in my soul that will never grow dim.

Prologue

I'm going to tell you this story and believe you me, it's true. So you just remember that when you feel your eyebrows rising and your mind saying, *She must be crazy*. It isn't crazy at all, it's just the truth. Might be hard to believe, but life is full of surprises, and you just never know what's coming your way.

Now, I know I never should have gone on such an adventurous walk in the first place. I mean I know I'm old, eighty-seven *is* getting old I suppose, but it doesn't mean I have to quit living, and I'm sick and tired of everyone expecting me to.

I had made my move, set my goal, and my mind was made up. For too long I'd been following the rules of the golden years. Rules put in place by those that have no idea what they're talking about. I'm sorry to say when the rule makers arrive at the golden years, they will most likely want to eat their words and change the rules. Unfortunately, it will be too late.

When you become my age, you look at life in a bit shorter segments than when you're younger. I quit planning by the decade a while ago. Now, I like to sit down with my calendar and figure out a year. One year at a time; which is exactly what I did.

The upcoming year would involve a departure from the imposed safety of the suffocating walls gracing my senior living apartment to the open air freedom of life found in my little slice of paradise.

Beginning with the on-set of fall, I would be living in my little cabin perched on the shore of my lovely mountain lake, a place I'd cherished for all the years of my existence; a place where the best things in my life happened, and unfortunately, the worse. Yet being there would bring me peace, I knew. And it was peace I needed to wash through my heart and soul. I was sure to find what was lost to me so long ago, and lose the burdens that continued to hold me down.

My burdens were heavy on my shoulders, burdens of guilt and sadness. I have seen them in the eyes of a demon deep in the dead of night many times over the years. I set out to rid myself of them and find the peace a person needs to end their days with. A peace that saturates body, mind, and soul.

So, my journey began with a list of what to bring, how much to bring, and who to tell, which ended up to be no one. Other than food and clothing and the normal things, I would bring my books, my music, and a nice new journal-one that I would use to chronicle the adventures I planned to have throughout the seasons of the coming year. I would fill it with memories and stories and words intended to be read by my family, particularly after I'm gone. Words that would remind them of the beauty and preciousness of life. Words that would remind them of what's important and what is not.

This was my plan and I could hardly wait to get started.

The Channel

As you get close to the lake, you can smell it—the scent of sun-drenched pine riding on the breeze, the musk of the earth. And then the sunshine streams through the dense forest and catches your eyes and you find yourself smiling with the knowledge that you're almost there. I remember how we rolled our windows all the way down as we got close just as I did the day I set out to spend the final seasons of my life in my cabin on the lake. No one ever wanted to miss out on the welcome that Mother Nature had planned for us. She touched our senses in so many ways—the smells, the sounds, the birds, and the breeze all there to welcome us. The children would have a contest to see who could see it first. Who would be the first to catch a glimpse of dancing sparkles on the water, to catch sight of a fishing boat in the channel or one going under the bridge? Who would be the first to see our little slice of paradise?

Now, from the road, the lakes were not visible, so the first water sighting was always of the channel. The channel connects the lower lake to the upper lake. It is an amazing wetland, full of bogs and water lilies, turtles, frogs, fish, and insects. It's a place were Herons and Cranes nest in the marshland along with hundreds of other birds. They twitter and chirp and sing and the insects buzz. Darn right noisy there, most of the time. And the water is always murky through the channel—murky, warm water just deep enough for folks to get their boats through so we could all go visiting from the upper lake to the lower lake.

One of my favorite things to do on quiet summer mornings was to take a cup of coffee in the little paddle boat and go through the channel so I could experience nature waking up before my own children woke up. It has been a while since I've been able to do that, but I so looked forward to doing it again when the good weather set in.

Anyway, the channel yawned and stretched and came to life a million ways in one. Water lilies, bright yellow and green, opened up and became room and board for gnats by the thousands. And turtles, all kinds of little snapping turtles, sunbathed on old deadheads stuck in the marsh and the mud. They would abandon ship and disappear into the murky water as I paddled on by. I imagine they were expecting to be captured if they lingered too long. Every summer the boys tried to convince all kinds of turtles that they were meant to be our pets. Of course, I always convinced the boys to let 'em go before the poor little things died and stunk up the cabin.

The birds of the channel sang the sweetest morning songs and took to the air after a smorgasbord of insects, more insects than they'd ever be able to eat in a life time. They were so graceful, swooping and gliding and diving. And then the water skimmers would flit across the top of the water, right into the wide open mouth of the bass. Breakfast for everyone.

As you can see, the world of the channel was different from the rest of the world. It was an education every day. It was also surprisingly humid in the channel where as it wasn't humid on either of the lakes. This has always been a mystery to us all.

Now the channel had some back alley types of water ways, like little secret passages, and one of them was my very favorite place to paddle because of where it led. It was a narrow passage with dense marsh on one side and a low bank on the other side. There were even a few little ramshackle cabins on the tucked away and overgrown bank for those folks who apparently really wanted their privacy. Sometimes I wondered how they even found their little places hidden away under all that foliage, beach grass up to your waist, and cattails as tall as Jack.

The wonderful thing about this passageway was the willow trees. There were three giant willows growing on the bank. Their branches reached all the way across the waterway and hung down, actually touching the marsh on the other side. You had to part a curtain of branches and leaves to paddle through an imaginary door, letting it swing shut behind you. Inside, you found yourself in a beautiful green gazebo, cool and pleasant and kind of mysterious and haunting too.

"Welcome," the willows whispered. "We've been expecting you."

"I got here as soon as I could," I would assure them.

I love the willows and the peaceful sanctuary they offered. I swear those willow trees talked to me, calmed me and soothed my soul while they tucked me away from the rest of the world. I always stopped my paddling for a while and just drifted around, enjoying the damp dark coolness, sipping my coffee and thanking God for allowing me to be there. And always I closed my eyes—closed my eyes so the willows could work their magic, gently brushing a leafy kiss across my face and a tender caress on my arms. Sometimes, I nearly cried at the beauty of it all.

The paddle boat is new now, much easier to maneuver than the old one. I planned to venture into the channel and under the tranquil canopy of the willows every day come summer. Every season is filled with it's own menu of unique gifts. I don't think I've ever looked forward to them as much as I did at that time of my life.

Now, as I mentioned, the channel even had its own kind of folks living there. Unique folks, not the sun worshiping noisy types like the rest of us. They were the quiet types that preferred life on the inside of their dwelling as opposed to life on the outside. There is even a ten-mile-per-hour speed limit through the channel to protect their tranquility. It's posted on each end, a reminder for when you're coming and for when you're going. Lord knows if anyone ever broke that speed limit and went ripping on through, the residents there would be on the phone to the water patrol in a heartbeat. They'd actually come and launch a boat and go cruising around looking for the offender. A ticket would be issued when the offender was discovered. I never knew of any of my darling children doing such a thing, yet I feel confident that they did.

On the north end of the channel was my beloved old bridge. On that particular day, I was just interested in taking a walk over the old wooden bridge. It had been so long, and it was calling to my very soul. I couldn't *not* go, and I had no intention of continuing up the old logging road. Somehow that just happened. But we'll talk about all that later.

As I was saying, in order to get to the lower lake by boat, you have to drive your boat through the channel and under the bridge. When the water level is high, the kids would stand up and try to touch the underside of the bridge as we passed through. It used to be a rickety old wooden bridge that was used by the hermit types living on the other side. They would drive over the bridge and then continue to their cabins by way of a very rutted out dirt road, no more than a sad little path, really. The road ran behind the cabins almost the whole length of the channel.

The bridge was only wide enough for one car at a time. Truth be told, I doubt very much that it could have remained standing under the weight of two cars at a time so it's a good thing it was so narrow. Most folks drove over that old bridge very cautiously, holding their breath and saying their prayers, and Jack and I would watch in wonder that it never collapsed. I swear you could see it sag under the weight. I never drove over that bridge myself, just walked over it. But if I'd ever had a reason to drive over it I always knew I'd do it fast. I always thought that going so slow was practically begging it to give way.

I loved that old bridge. It's all new now. I hardly recognized it that day I took my walk. A new bridge without any history or character or squeaky rickety charm. It's a safe bridge now, still only wide enough for one car at a time, but wide enough for a walker on each side and a car all together. It looks a lot more trustworthy, I will admit, although I don't know why they always have to ruin everything with the ever-so-glamorous, new and improved models.

I'm sure some folks would like to see me replaced with a new and improved model. A new Adeline, one that doesn't cause such a load of worry for the family. *What would they like me to do?* I often wonder. *Just quit dreaming?* I guess if you don't have your dreams, you don't really have a life, and then no one would have cause to worry, that's for sure.

Well, as you know, that's not for me. Not for the likes of Adeline Leanne McGrath-Cornell, and that's for sure.

The Road

Now, the road leading to the lake was steep and narrow, winding and twisting with hairpin turns on one side and steep cliffs dropping straight down into the deepest parts of the lake on the other. It was a dangerous road that demanded one's undivided attention.

The Bible says those who chose the narrow road, the road less traveled, will find life and I believe this to be true. My life was found every summer at the end of this long, narrow road, difficult and less traveled as it was. Everyone who summered there believed their lives were found at the end of that horrible road provided we got there all in one piece. Unfortunately, there were a few who lost their lives along the way, driving off the cliffs in an alcohol-induced stupor deep in the dead of night. But there was no other way to get there. There'd be no straightening the road. How could that be done? As long as a person was sober and minded the speed limit, which was twenty impossibly slow miles per hour, everything would be fine.

But, of course, our little lakeside community had its share of fools just like everywhere else in the world, and I'm sorry to report that many a car had careened off the cliffs over the years.

I imagine there's a whole wrecking yards worth of rusted out automobiles sitting at the bottom of the lake right now. I often wonder if the big fish get the big cars. Once, it swallowed up a bus. I'll bet the sturgeon get to live in that.

Anyway, alcohol was always the cause, naturally. Not the intoxicated drivers mind you, but the alcohol itself. If only it would leave us summer folk alone.

How to improve the safety of our community as we all traveled to and fro by way of the devil road was discussed at the annual home owners meeting each June. Our road was a conundrum; did we love it or did we hate it? It was the yellow brick road, the road to paradise, yet it was the road from hell, a lying snake of a road. It seemed that every year we allocated a little more money to put up even more guard rails and red flashers—guard rails that cars would career right on through and flashers that would fail to warn a person of their dangerous flirtation with the cliffs as they sped around the corners and felt the gravelly edge slip away beneath their tires.

It didn't seem to matter what we did or how much we cautioned. What is it in human nature that causes a person to ignore the truth? Why do so many pretend to be surprised when the terrifying inevitable occurs?

I guess most folks just figure bad things will never happen to them, especially when they're young.

Following the annual meeting we'd all get together for potluck and serve each other cheap wine and Schlitz Beer. Later, the music would start and all the old people (that would be anyone over thirty years of age) would gather up their leftovers and scramble out like a plague was heading our way—hurry home before the loud rock and roll music infected our very senses and brainwashed us as it evidently had our children; hurry home before we lost our hearing and

our minds; hurry home before the inky darkness settled on the unsettling road.

The young people, of course, danced and drank
the night away, oblivious to the danger they refused to
acknowledge or to accept. They were just young and
full of romantic anticipation for the warm summer
evenings that lay ahead. I guess I understood them. I
remember being young, a long, long time ago.

Sometime before sunrise, as the campfires finally
died out and exhaustion took hold of their bodies,
they would wander on home, some of them walking,
some of them driving. It didn't matter which they
were doing; they were in danger all the same.

The road confused the drivers who were most
assuredly under a variety of bad influences, and the
walkers stumbled in the ruts and crumbling asphalt.
Our prayers alone, I have no doubt, are what brought
them home in one piece.

Regardless of the menace, it was a magical place
and a magical time of our lives. I loved everything
about it—the warm night air, the camp fires, the silly
songs, and terrible guitar playing. And the presence
of the moon. Oh, that glorious moon. I will carry the
moon inside me forever. A globe so enormous ris-

ing over the mountains casting shadows and mystery everywhere you looked.

Sometimes at night I would wake up to find the moon rising late, rising up from the back side of the dark, looming mountains.

"Adie," Jack would whisper, "Why are you awake?"

"Why are you awake, Jack?" I asked in return. I could hear his smile.

I would watch the moon from the warmth of our bed as it crept slowly across the sky. It illuminated everything as it went: the neighboring cabins, the boats lying still in their liquid bed, the infinite canopy of evergreens, and the wonderful barn owls on the fence post hooting softly into the night.

"I can't help it, Jack. It's the moon." And we would spoon a little tighter.

The mountains linked together their outstretched arms like giants in a huddle and surrounded the black bowl of a lake keeping us cocooned against the rest of the world.

"It *is* a beautiful moon, Addie," Jack would mutter, sighing deeply.

Loons made their presence known, mournful and beautiful, sending shivers down my spine as they called across the still waters to each other, called to their mates to be found in the night while making delicate splashes on the surface of the water; water so still I swear it was possible to see the tracks of a mosquito skip across the top in that moonlight.

And always, hiding under the surface of everything beautiful lie the dangers of the never-ending road—a road to make you crazy, a road of confusion, yet one that led to a sanctuary so intricately woven into our very souls that we willingly risked everything for it, time and time again.

I shivered. "Trevor will be driving in another year, Jack." But Jack was asleep.

Spring Cleaning

Well now, the lower lake was a long, skinny body of water that curved back and forth like a snake. It was of course connected to the upper lake by the channel. Our cabin sat on the far side of the upper lake, and it was shaped like a bowl... the lake, that is, not the cabin. The cabin, well I'll get to that in a bit.

Now the lower lake had a charm all it's own, what with all the twisting and turning. But most importantly, the lower lake was the location of the famous rope swing and of the diving cliffs. A white wooden cross graced the hill above the cliffs as a reminder that someone had tragically died at some time in history jumping off those cliffs.

If you think that was a reasonable warning for people like us, you are wrong. We jumped anyway. Not only did we jump off the death defying cliffs, we climbed up the trunk of an old falling down tree, hung onto a shredding knotted up old rope, and swung out over the water. We would let go with a scream just as we cleared the jutting rocks that threatened to break our bodies into pieces if we let go too soon. It was the thrill of it all, you know, and even though we occasionally had a close call or two, it only seemed to sweeten the deal, if you can believe it. I guess you could say we were an adventurous sort, if not a bit crazy.

Now, as I said, our cabin sat on the far side of the upper lake. The upper lake was preferable because of its shape. You were better off water skiing on the wide open upper lake, and it tended to be a lot calmer than the lower lake, yet it was not without its share of interesting shoreline, coves and points, and even a fresh water mountain spring that we often filled our water jugs from. The upper lake was protected by surrounding mountains covered in towering evergreens and thick heavy foliage. Pine and fir trees were everywhere; all kinds of berries grew, and wild roses blossomed all summer long. We had a paradise, we did.

All I set out to do was to experience the seasons one more time in my little heaven on earth. And all I wanted to do that day was take a walk in the crisp fall air and visit my beloved old bridge.

Anyway, first I need to let you know how the cabin came to be. You see, with the babies coming along and business just getting started, Jack did what a father has to do in order to build his family a summertime home. He always said he'd never have his children wasting away in the city all summer long when they could be running wild at the lake. So he salvaged materials from demolition projects. Sometimes people would call him up and say, "Hey, if you want some doors or some paneling or whatever before the so and so building gets knocked down, go get it." And Jack would drop everything and run off ahead of the wrecking ball and take what he could. Consequently, each room in our cabin had its own unique style; different wallboard or paneling, different doors, different shapes and sizes. He would just make adjustments and get the materials to fit together as best he could.

As you might imagine, we had perhaps a little better ventilation in that old cabin than was ideal.

And oh my, the variety of windows! We had some amazing windows and some windows without any glass or with cracked glass, and we even had a tiny stained glass one. Jack cut a hole in the wall at the end of the hallway and put it there so we could all enjoy the way the sun shone through the colors in the morning light, painting rainbows everywhere we looked.

In our bathroom, we had a very old-fashioned commode with a pull chain flusher that Jack rescued from an old hotel in the process of taking its last breath. I was proud to have it grace our quaint little bathroom, but I have always worried about the weight of it and the chance of it falling through the floor. If it did, you see, it would most likely land on my head while I worked away in the kitchen. I'm not sure what Jack used for flooring, and I'm sure I don't want to know.

As a contrast, and for the sake of keeping things interesting, a very modern, bright pink bathtub kept company with the commode and then there was a sink, of course. Just a plain ole sink, nothing remarkable about it.

Now the door never fit quite right, which caused all kinds of frustration, especially with the girls, even when Jack would try and fix it here and there all the time. There was always the feeling of exposure in that little bathroom. The only good thing about that is nobody spent any unnecessary time in there. That was a blessing over the years as there were nine of us all together back then. Oh, Lord, that was a lot of people sharing one tiny little bathroom. I sometimes wonder how we did it.

The cabin, as you might imagine, was a sieve of a summer dwelling few folks would bother to construct and although we didn't intend to lay out the welcome mat for every rodent within a hundred mile radius, apparently that's just exactly what we did.

The mice spent the winters nice and cozy, nesting in the dresser drawers and between the springs of the old mattresses. Opening up the cabin for the season was always a day of mixed emotions, excitement for the onset of summer and dread for what surprises were waiting to be discovered. More times than I can count, we'd uncover newborn mice, all pink and squeaky, in a nest of toilet paper scraps, squirming together for warmth.

I'd get Jack and the kids to haul the mattresses outside so we could beat them like old rugs. I'd have the boys get sticks and go at it, encouraging the unwelcomed inhabitants of the stuffing to scurry out and run for their lives. The mattresses always smelled like mouse. We were either successful in getting rid of the smell or we just got used to it, I never was sure which. But I'll tell you one thing for sure, after a day of beating those old things around and airing them out in the warm sun, we'd happily drop our weary bones down to sleep on any one of them.

Next, I'd remove any dresser drawers the stinky trespassers had chosen as a nursery and dump the naked pink contents into the icy rushing waters of the neighboring creek. The creek normally overflowed with the heavy snow melt off coming from the mountain backing up the cabin. Although each spring the boys begrudgingly dug out a trench around the back of our humble structure, there was always flood damage that resulted in a thick layer of silt carpeting the cabin floor. I'd get the boys to start by shoveling out as much as they could by scraping the big flat face of a snow shovel across the old wooden floor and out the front door. Then they'd use the sorry remains of an old push broom to remove what the shovel didn't get. I'd finish off with two or three good moppings. By that time we'd all agree it was good as new.

Next, we'd attempt to plump up the rock hard sand bags edging the creek, adding a stack of rocks here and there, just in case there was a final overflow before the snow was completely melted high in the mountains. These things together would hopefully save us from having to do the floor a second time. It usually worked, but sometimes it didn't.

There were always unexpected surprises to deal with too. Once there was a dead bobcat rotting away under the porch and smelling so bad we didn't know if we'd ever get rid of that stench. Occasionally a dead bat was hanging around somewhere, usually off the fabric cover of a front room chair or off the draperies. At least they were dead. Spiders, dead and alive, inhabited every possible nook and cranny and, for some reason, the bath tub by the dozens. Not understanding what the attraction was, we reasoned that the live ones spent their time in there surviving off the dead ones.

The windows would all get washed and the shutters would be removed. When that was done, you could see crystal clear all the way to the end of the lake. The shutters didn't open and close properly, so it was just easier to remove them completely and then nail them back up in the fall. We saved the removal job for the middle of June though, knowing the weather would most likely cooperate after then.

Our spring cleaning was always topped off by using the entire contents of a can of Lysol Disinfectant Spray. The idea was that we'd leave our summer home not only de-moused, de-bugged, and de-mudded, but disinfected too. Eventually, we'd have the place looking and smelling livable, and we'd leave trusting to return the next weekend to things just as we'd left them. A pipe dream, of course.

Oh my, I miss those times.

Mother Earth

I was a rarity. That's what Jack called me. A rarity.

"Momma, where are you going? Can I come with you?"

"No, Itsy, you need to stay home. I'm taking a momma break."

Itsy hated it when I walked off alone. She was a growth on my hip, that child was.

"Itsy, you stay with me," Jack called her. "Let your momma have a little break now. Let's go swimming with the others, you and me." Jack would take her by the hand and join the rest of the kids at the water.

"Don't you go too far now, Adie," he'd holler over his shoulder, dragging Itsy along.

She'd look back with watery eyes, stumbling her way to the lake. "Don't be so long that I worry."

"There's nothing out there to worry about, Jack. I'll be along." And I'd wander away from the cabin and walk in the woods all alone. I was never afraid, just in love with how different it was from the rest of the world, in love with what it had to offer if you just went looking. I liked to feel the earth breathe around me and the trees whisper as a light breeze blew on through; blew gently through the bows and passed softly through the needles so that the trees whistled a breathy quiet whistle. It was a serenade from the giants of the forest, a lullaby. I always walked deep into the forest, hiking up old trails that led to more old trails. I never found the end of them without ending up on the other side of the mountain. That's how far they went. The pine scent invaded my nostrils, sticky like and sweet. It would last for days, as if my sinuses were coated with a fine pine film. It was intoxicating to me.

There was a small but steady stream that meandered through the forest, refreshing everything in its path, watering the earth. Eventually it made its way to the lake like a long, sleepy snake winding around the forest under fallen trees and layers of brush; a lazy stream, one with all the time in the world.

Up the trails I would go, taking my sweet time and feeling my mind empty as I attached my senses to the beauty surrounding me. If I hadn't had Jack and the children to take care of, I do believe I would have simply become one with the forest. I loved it so much.

After a time, the trail would level off a bit and would come to a clearing all drenched in sunshine. I loved to lie down on the soft, warm forest floor, heated and well padded with a thick layer of leaves and pine needles, soft and musty from the heat of the day. I knew it had been put there special, just for me. I would close my eyes and stretch out my arms and legs to feel as much of the earth as I could, feel it under my flesh and my bones. I would hear the soft whistle of the pine trees singing, soak up the warmth from above and below me, inhale the power and force of the earth. She spoke to me, comforted me, let me know that one day I would be one with her, a part of her and the trees and the lazy stream. I've never been afraid of death because of the understanding I have with my earth and with my God. The earth will take care of my body, and the Lord will take care of my soul. And I would be struck with knowing that there was no other place like this on earth. And I felt sorry for everyone that wasn't us, that would never experience what we had, what I had those times all to myself.

I remember one time I removed my clothing. Yes, I did. I needed the touch of the earth on my flesh so badly, desperately. I lay down naked, ground into the cradle of the earth as tightly as I could fit and felt it move my body. My blood flowed as the power of nature moved it through my veins. My bed was lined with soft, warm pine needles and leaves and moss just green enough to be tender on my skin. I felt its heartbeat, the heartbeat of Mother Nature and her breathing, like a steadily building earthquake, slowly rumbling under the earth's crust.

I felt my heart slow and my breath fall in sync with the gentle rise of the earth as she inhaled. And then, as she exhaled, my spine seamed to curve into the cradle of her arms and she held me close and warmed my body and my soul. Tears of contentment ran down my face to mix with the part of me I was leaving behind with mother earth that day. I have felt such power, such life and passion in few instances, childbirth being one of them, and the night I spent on the mountain, being the other. On *that* night I was more acutely alive than I have ever been, yet at the same time, I have never ridden so closely on the cusp of death.

Dreams

I was thinking about that storm, Beanie. You remember, don't you? The famous storm that brought that huge old cypress down on Macmillan's barn, way up at the head of the lake? I'm sure you were there, even though I don't know as I saw you.

Anyway, for some reason I've been thinking about it a lot these days, although I wish I weren't.

I remember that day how the water got so murky and dark, the wind blowing so crazy, churning everything up with the waves. And the sky was growing darker by the minute. Huge thunder clouds rolled in like rogue waves threatening to swallow us up. Clouds black as coal and daggers of lightning slicing the sky in flashes so quick they were gone in a blink of the eye. Were they ever really there?

There was daylight, although it was fading, glowing through the wild waters over my head. Looking up I saw the ripple of the wind skimming over the surface and then waves rolling over me, drowning out the ripples. Then the clouds started shrinking the blue in the sky, and I knew it wouldn't be long before total darkness overtook me. I needed to get to the surface as quickly as I could, but I was looking for you, Beanie. Where were you?

The oxygen was escaping my lungs, and I was frantically searching for you, clawing my way through the murkiness, my heart pounding and my ears ringing. The water was getting colder and colder. I didn't know how long I could stand to stay in. Would I actually leave you behind? I cried so hard that my tears filled the lake and soon, it flooded the skiff. I'd given up holding on to it when I dove down to pull you out. Now it was beside me, a little skiff with a seat for both of us if we would just come on board. I grabbed for an oar that was drifting to the surface. How would we paddle out without an oar?

But soon, the skiff drifted to the bottom and I could no longer see it. It's possible it went to pick you up. I don't really know. But I knew one thing for sure, I needed to breathe. A heavy weight was pressing on my chest and I was gasping. I tried to swim to the surface but something was keeping me down.

I was happy that God had sent the skiff for you because I was useless; I was drowning.

I was so frozen with fear I couldn't move, terrified of staying and terrified of leaving you alone. If only you could have signaled me from the safety of above. Maybe you could have been swimming or paddling in a little float and you could have waved your arms over the water and I would have seen your strawberry hair and your tanned skin and the honesty of your smile. I would have known that you were all right then and I would have felt free to leave, and then I wouldn't have had to see it. I would have been able to rise to the surface and catch my breath, truly a breath of life. But it didn't happen that way, did it Beanie? It didn't happen so simply, as it seems life never really does. So many road blocks, so many complications in such a simple plan—at least what started out to be a simple plan anyway. This life, you know, I don't believe it was ever meant to be so difficult. Did it become this way because of us or in spite of us?

So I wasn't free from my demon after all. I'd been overly confident so it came as quite a surprise.

My guard was down, and I was rolling with the thunder and suddenly, there it was, holding me under, keeping me a prisoner of terrifying guilt and sadness. Reminding me to pay close attention in life, close attention to those you love or you just might lose them along the way just as I had lost you. I could hear it's mockery of ugly laughter ringing in my ears.

My lungs ached from the abrupt suction of air; they couldn't fill up fast enough. So out of breath, I was nearly done for. It ached—it did—to fill them up so quickly, so desperately, yet it was all I could do to keep myself alive, then I did what I could to calm myself, to slow my racing heart and ease the ache in my chest. But most of all, it was all I could do to get the tragedy out of my sight. I couldn't sit in silence for fear that the quiet would fill up with the anguished sounds of your mother's cries and your father's agony. There was nothing to do but pray.

I never really recovered from that storm, Beanie. I only turned my back on it knowing I would have to face it all again one day. But when the time came and I finally did, I knew I would be done with it forever. I would finally find peace.

But Jack needed me right then. For the first time in our lives, I was the one to lead the way. And I did. I only wish he would have followed close behind. I only wish he'd had the strength to keep up.

Ordinary Day

You know, Beanie, I woke one ordinary morning for no other reason than to make my way through another ordinary day and decided right then and there that I could no longer justify my ever-so ordinary existence. I had become so cautious there was no life left in my living. I took inventory of myself that day starting with my physical being.

The mirror doesn't lie, you know, and what I saw wasn't connected in any way to who I am. I stood in front of the mirror like an old witch, eyes sinking into my skull, the color nearly used up and gone. I scared myself.

I smiled at the witch and she smiled back—teeth all there. That was good news. A bit yellowed and larger than I ever remembered. Must be receding gums. Now if I went to a dentist, he would probably tell me I needed a gum surgery before they are completely receded and start to fall out of my head. It's a good thing I don't bother with the dentist anymore at my age.

The next thing I examined was my lovely neck. Nothing less than a swan's neck, you know. It looked like a long, skinny piece of gnarled driftwood with a big knob on one end which was my head and a sunken chest on the other. The sunken chest had two wrinkly old arms sticking out on either side, and I do believe the claws attached at the end used to be my lovely hands.

And then there was my bottom, which used to be quite nice back in the day. Have you ever studied the rear end of an elephant, Beanie? Notice the saggy, baggy flesh hanging down to the knees of the beast? Well, I suppose you get the picture.

Speaking of knees, mine didn't look well that day. They were kind of red and inflamed looking, liver spots here and there decorating my skin like sloppy brown polka dots. My eyes traveled down the crooked line of myself and ended up at my feet. You wouldn't believe how cute my feet used to be, but not anymore. What I beheld at the end of my legs was just awful. What in the world ever happened to my pretty feet? The bunion on my left foot has gotten large as the knuckle on the big toe of an ape. No wonder my feet would rather I just stay off them these days.

All in all, Beanie, I just couldn't deny there wasn't really any reason to hang on to it—this body I mean. It's time had come and gone. I might as well try living extraordinarily, if it were still possible, and use it up. I had always thrown caution to the wind and done whatever I chose. But you know, you chose differently when your body gets so tired and everything you do makes you stiff and sore. I think the mind slows down because the body does. I had begun the downhill slide; that was for sure. There is no reason to sit back on one's laurels and wait for the body to give out. I decided that day to follow my heart and my mind and if my old body couldn't keep up, well, at least it would die trying.

I decided right then and there to move to the cabin for one year. I planned to be there to enjoy each of the seasons one more time, while I still could. My days were numbered, that was for sure, so I would begin right then, in the crimson and golden beauty of the fall. Fall was already well on it's way, everything in nature preparing for the wind and the cold and the rain. Yet I knew there would also be days of spectacular sunshine with gentle winds sweeping fallen leaves high into the sky like crisp and golden confetti against a backdrop of brilliant blue.

And I started dreaming about how I'd be there to welcome old man winter. I could just see it; snow flurries and ice cycles and the lake freezing over. Families would show up on the weekends to skate and sled and I'd have visitors for a while. And I'd read all the classics I've not gotten around to while sipping tea and stoking the fire.

Suddenly, my minds eye held a vision of blue bells and buttercups and all the other wild flowers as they raise their arms to the sun while spring showers bring everything to life. And butterflies would emerge from their cocoons and all the babies of the forest would be born. Tiny birds would learn to fly and little squirrels would race up and down the trees, fresh with new leaves. And I'd be there to witness it all.

Come summer, my solitude would surely come to an end. I have no doubt that there would not be a single day to enjoy on my own. But then, that's what I really loved the most. Those warm sunny days. The birds singing in the morning and motor boats pulling water skiers all after noon. And then the evenings filled with the smell and crackle of campfires.

But most of all, I would enjoy my memories there, reliving all the wonderful times we had. And I would relive the sad times too. The times my heart can't seem to let go of.

So, much to everyone's dismay, I began to live again in my favorite place in the world. I know in my heart that I was doing what I needed to do.

I hardly recognized the place any longer, your momma and everyone fixing it up like they have. I'm not saying it's not nice and all, Beanie, but I preferred it the old way. For goodness' sakes, I hear there's even a window washer that shows up now and then. A window washer!

Anyway, I know they were all getting ready to take my car keys away soon, so I needed to get out to the cabin and plant myself before they could stop me. I am still the legal owner after all, and if I wanted to spend the seasons or even the rest of my life there, I certainly had a right to do just that.

Lord, Beanie. Run for your life when you get this old, because the world wants nothing more than to stop you dead in your tracks. Is it better, I wonder, by worldly standards, to die in an easy chair watchin' Wheel of Fortune, or to die having an adventure? Well, we all know the answer to that. So throw a rock at the idiot box and get out the door fast, before they slam it in your face, locking you in.

Now, as I was saying, I packed up and went to the cabin feeling like a kid running away from home. My excitement was so overwhelming; I had to force myself to concentrate on my driving. All I could think of was how happy I was and how wonderful it was all going to be. I brought plenty of warm clothes for the fall nights. It would be a shame not to spend them outside, and I brought plenty of groceries for one. I had my hands full when I got there but I must say, it was so much fun opening the place up again and being there alone. No one telling me to sit down and let them do it. I loved that it was all up to me once again.

I knew it was just closed up since Labor Day and there weren't mice or muddy floors or dead things around anymore. My goodness, I will admit it was a bit of a relief to simply turn on the water and flip the switch on the hot water tank and have everything so nice and clean. I put my bread and vegetables in the refrigerator and soups in the cupboard. There were still a lot of canned goods in there, some tuna and stewed tomatoes. I found a couple cans of oysters. That would be from your Uncle Tim, you know. He loves those canned oysters. There were a few cans of pie filling. I thought I might make myself a cherry pie and eat the whole thing myself. I giggled out loud at the thought of it.

Well, I spent the first night there outside sleeping on my nice wooden lounger, the one they've been trying to use for firewood for the past ten years. I got out the cushions and some quilts and pillows and made the nicest little bed. I positioned it right under my favorite tree—that great big cedar hovering over the side of the cabin. Then I put on my warmest flannels and wool socks and even a stocking hat so my body heat wouldn't escape out from the top of my head, my hair being as thin as it is these days. I talked to God all night long. He put the constellations on display and plenty of shooting stars too. Fall nights are the best time to watch a show of shooting stars, you know.

The moon rose over the lake very late that night and reflected off the still water, illuminating everything around me. The neighboring cabins were so quiet and still, not a soul around. There were only a few boats left in the water, most folks having taken them out Labor Day. I noticed our little Boston Whaler was out already. I wished it wasn't. I would have loved to launch it, but I would probably regret it, maybe forgetting to put the plug in or some such thing. I would certainly never hear the end of that.

When, I wonder, did my children become so old? Why had they allowed the world to ruin their adventurous souls? Sometimes I cry for the loss of their youth more so than I have ever cried for my own. They had such beautiful spirits, full of the need to explore the earth and nature and all it offers, full of anticipation to take on the world. I wonder how long it's been since any one of my adult children has slept outside just to spend the night under the stars, talking to God? Do they remember the moon and the night sounds? Do they long for the cry of the loons?

I don't know why I ever allowed myself to be separated from what is real. I decided that night, sleeping outside with the earth and Mother Nature and God, that I would never be separated again.

I slept some that night, waking to the sun rising up from behind the mountains, painting the sky brilliant pinks and oranges and purples before it peeked its head over the top and began the process of waking up the world with its brilliance and warmth. This was the way to start a day in an extraordinary way. I was so pleased with myself for being there, and I decided it was okay to sleep for the morning. After all, I hadn't slept much that night. Maybe my nights would become my days. They were much more interesting, that's for sure.

I closed my eyes and slept the most peaceful quiet sleep I've ever had, waking only because my stomach was growling. I took my time getting on my feet, feeling the cold layer of dew dampening my quilts and my face. I realized the opportunity to sleep out under the stars would be drawing to an end as the nights would soon grow colder. I would need to take advantage of the short time I had left.

There were no sounds whatsoever, the silence so dense; simply slipping my feet into my damp slippers and shuffling to the door was disturbing to nature. I went inside and put the kettle on, shivering a bit from the cold morning air. I put two slices of bread in the toaster and decided to start a fire in the wood-burning stove. My, it was surprising to feel fall in the air so intensely.

It was an easy stove to get going and as always, it heated the place up in a hurry. I struggled to remove the lid on a fresh jar of raspberry jam and then slathered it on my toast. That's my favorite, you know. I still had a chill for some reason, so I wrapped up in a blanket and curled up in the rocking chair by the stove and had my breakfast. Sometime, I don't know when, I fell back to sleep. When I woke, I was surprised to see my toast was gone, as was my coffee. I didn't really remember breakfast but apparently, I had eaten it. My neck was stiff from sleeping in the chair, and I needed to use the restroom so I decided to take a shower and get properly dressed for the day. By that time, it was getting on in the afternoon, and I had it in mind to take a good long walk before it got too late in the day. You see, I'd forgotten how the days were getting shorter and I wouldn't have light late into the evening like we'd had all summer long. Lord, things change in a hurry. I felt that we'd just started daylight saving time and here we were getting ready to lose it again. Or had we lost it already? I couldn't remember.

I hurried to get ready, eating a banana for a late lunch. Not much, I admit, but I wasn't particularly hungry. I guess by the time I left the cabin, it must have been about three in the afternoon. I really don't know. But I was wearing my good walking shoes and my light wool jacket, and I was feeling like a young girl all over again. So excited I was, at the prospect of heading down the road, off on an adventure of my own. Maybe there'd be some fisherman in the channel or turtles sunbathing on logs. You just never knew what would be waiting for you.

Stepping into the shade was a hearty welcome to fall. What a nip there was in the air. But the sunshine was warm and bright. I put my sunglasses on and started down the drive. The road would be safe to walk down this time of year, with no one here but me. I wondered seriously if I would see a single soul other than myself. It was my goal to walk across the old bridge crossing the channel. That would be a good walk for such a wonderful afternoon.

Did you know I found a pair of old gloves in one of my pockets? I don't even know whose they are, but they were good to have.

Not a soul was out, Beanie. You could hear a pin drop, I swear. My footsteps were loud on the gravely side of the road, crunching under my feet. It would be nice to say hello to a neighbor or two but by the looks of things, everyone was gone. They were missing the best season to be here, I decided. I walked along the road, wondering how it was that it never fell over the edge. I was careful not to get too close where it was steep. Not a single car passed, not a single person did I see. It was just me and the birds and squirrels. A beautiful hawk flew overhead, its shadow looming over the road. I looked up ahead at the bend. There would be four full bends in the road before reaching the tiny road leading over the old bridge.

The Walk

Mary Millers' garden had the largest dinner plate dahlias I've ever seen, all in brilliant colors. How could she leave them and move into town? I decided I'd pick me a bouquet on the way back. No sense in letting them go to waste. I'd have dahlias on the kitchen table and out on the picnic table too.

I walked by Old Man Moser's place and noticed his mailbox had been knocked over again. It was just in a bad spot, and I'll never understand why he didn't just move it. Oh, well. I think he may be dead now so it really doesn't matter. It looked like someone had been there though, because the garage door was part way opened. No car that I could see. My, but the yard had become overgrown. His wife—do you remember Lilly Moser, Beanie? She was the sweetest woman and a wonderful gardener. She'd be so sad to see the place looking that way.

Thompson's place was as immaculate as ever. Not a weed to be seen. I swear they've painted the place again. I've never seen *any* house painted so many times. Always looks so fresh and new. I wonder if the inside looks like that too. All these years and I never once saw the inside of that house. Not the most neighborly, those people.

Well, Stan and Willie's old cat, Ollie, was sitting on the wicker rocker on their back porch. I assumed that meant they'd just left for a short time and would be back soon. They never go anywhere without that cat. Maybe they decided to stay a while longer and enjoy the fall. Maybe I wasn't the only person there after all. If that was the case, I'd pick some dahlias for Willie too. Wouldn't Mary Miller be pleased to see us all enjoying her dahlias so?

At that moment, the sun broke from behind a cloud and the tin roof on Henry's old place lit up like it was on fire. I've always had a special place in my heart for Henry. Did you ever meet his wife, Beanie? You may have been too young. Her name was Esther, and she was a beautiful woman and very unusual. She was some kind of mix, you know? Like maybe she was part white and part black and part something else. Kept to herself most of the time. She was pretty shy.

Anyway, Henry adored her; it was evident in his eyes every time you saw him and said, "Say hello to Esther for me." He'd just light up at the sound of her name. Now, how a woman so loved and adored can up and leave a man like that and never be seen again is beyond me. But that's what happened. They never had any children—Esther and Henry. I never knew why, whether it was by choice or by fate. Yet they always seemed happy together. And then one day, after twenty-five years or so of being married to dear sweet Henry, Esther just packs up and goes one day. She left a note of good bye and that was that. The cabin took on Henry's mourning in its appearance. It's been an abandoned shell ever since she left. It's kind of a haunted looking place anyway, what with it being built out of rock and hidden back in the trees like it is. The wooden table and chairs still sit out on the side porch, although they're warped by the weather and most assuredly not suited for use any longer. But that Henry. He wore sorrow like nobody's business. I think there was a silent sigh of relief when he packed up and left one day too. It was such a burden on everyone's heart to so much as look at the man.

I heard he sold the house in town and moved back to the Midwest, where he's from, to be with family there. Maybe some siblings or such. But why he's never sold the cabin I'll never understand. Houses need to be lived in and when they're not, they end up looking just like Henry's place, forlorn and forgotten. It seems the structure is creeping away from the water a little bit each year, like it's retreating into the forest. The giant evergreens are so overgrown that you have to really look hard to spot a house hidden in there. The red shutters are barely red, fading into the color of the rock walls. It's pretty much all gray now. On a rainy day, you can't see the place at all. That house is disappearing just like Esther did. Poor Henry. I wonder if he's still alive and if his heart ever found peace. I do hope so.

There was the nicest scent in the air that day. You know, that early fall scent that tells you old man winter's on the way. Kind of hints at what the future holds, doesn't it? Kind of exciting because we never really know; just that a change is coming our way and we have no say in what that change will bring.

It struck me that I hadn't noticed how much fire wood was seasoned for the winter, yet there was normally quite a bit. I'd have to look into that when I got back as I planned to have a fire every day all winter long.

Well, nature has her way of keeping us on our toes, even if they are swollen up ole gnarly toes, like mine have become. I was aware of how good my feet felt that day. No problems in walking the distance I set out to walk. No pain in my knees or hips. I was so happy and feeling so fine. And free. Oh, Beanie, I felt as free as I've ever felt in my life on that beautiful day.

Well, I rounded the last bend and headed on down the little road leading over the bridge. All the cabins were closed up, looking peaceful and content, like they'd been wrapped up in a nice cozy blanket so they could hibernate for the winter. The sun was shining and warming my face as I took my time strolling down the gravel road. I've always felt it was more of a driveway than a road, it's so short and narrow. The water level was still low, so the boulders on both sides of the bridge were exposed more than normal. I could see sunfish darting in and out of the rocks.

Now, I have something to tell you, Beanie. When I started across the bridge, the strangest thing happened. I got to the middle of the bridge, walking very slowly as I was feeling strangely vulnerable right then, and I stopped and stared down into the water. It was so still and silent I felt like I was the only person on the planet and my reflection was as crystal clear as looking into a mirror. And there you were. Standing right beside me. I held my eyes steady on the reflection in the water and I smiled at you, Beanie, and you smiled right back. And then I reached for your hand and we were holding hands, smiling at each other, and that's when I felt my heart break. And that whole terrible day came crashing down around me. I had to sit down on the wooden planks of the bridge while my mind played out the whole ugly scene.

Why did it have to happen, Beanie? Why didn't I stop you from going? I'd had a bad feeling all along. If only I'd listened to the warning in my heart.

Jenny Lee

Jack loved nothing more than to watch his children parent their youngsters. He spent all his time chuckling and thinking up things to do with you grandkids for the sake of spoiling you all and annoying your parents to death. He always said they had it coming and he never felt sorry one bit. That is, until *that* day, Beanie, until that horrible day.

You were such a beautiful child, Jelly Bean, with tiny wisps of reddish hair and golden skin. And I could tell from the first time I held you in my arms and you looked straight into my eyes that you and I would have a special connection, because you were just like me. If there is mischief to be seen in an infant's twinkle of an eye, I saw it in yours, and I had to laugh. We connected right then and there, Jenny Lee, right then and there.

I've missed you so.

You know, when Itsy was pregnant with you, she ate jelly beans until we thought she'd turn into one. That girl had them stashed everywhere you can imagine, in her car, in her purse, in the bathroom cabinet, right next to the bathroom tissue for goodness' sake. It's a wonder she didn't weigh five hundred pounds what with all the sugar she took in during her pregnancy with you.

Well, I don't really know exactly how it came to be, but somehow, right after you were born, Jenny Lee became Jelly Bean and the next thing you know, your daddy and your Grandpa Jacks got everyone shortening it up to "Beanie." Your daddy said you were as cute and sweet as a little Jelly Bean and since that's what you were made of, that's what you should be called. It suited you just fine and you never seemed to mind. In fact, I often wondered if you even knew what your given name was. From Jenny Lee to Beanie, just like that.

Your poor momma, she tried to get everyone to call you by your real name, but it was too much fun to just say Beanie. So that's what we did. But we all knew when you were in trouble, now didn't we? That's the only time I'd ever hear your daddy holler "Miss Jenny Lee!" When he called out for Miss Jenny Lee, we all thought, *Run and hide, Beanie.* We may not have known what you did, but one thing we knew for sure was you were in trouble.

And oh, how you stole our hearts away, little girl. You especially knew just how to get to your grandpa's heart. He would have done anything in the world for you, Beanie. But what he did for you was end your life.

That's not how anyone *else* saw it, that's for sure, but that's how Jack saw it. It breaks my heart into a million pieces when I think about that day. I put it out of my mind for a good long time, you know, so I don't understand what happened or why, but that day on the bridge, it all came crashing down around me, and there it was. I don't know how long I sat there and cried, but I cried my heart out, for you, for Jack, for all of us.

Nothing was ever the same after that. No one wanted to be there any longer. I did though. I knew you didn't blame your grandpa or anything else. It was an accident, but my Lord, what a terrible accident.

And wasn't it such a silly thing? Jack was always looking for ways to entertain you grandkids, and you all loved to ride on anything that we could pull behind the boat. Well, Jack had been keeping his eye out for something all of you kids could ride on at once, all together, you know? So, when his pilot friend called to say he had an airplane fuel tank that he figured about six kids could fit on at one time, Jack was thrilled. The tank was about ten feet long and two feet tall and about three to four feet wide. Empty of gasoline, it would float forever, as long as the valve was kept shut tight. The valve was on the bottom side of the tank and stuck out about five inches. All Jack could think about was hooking up that tank and pulling all the grandkids around the lake. It would be like a toboggan for the water instead of the snow. He was so excited to get it. I have to say though, it was the ugliest thing I've ever seen floating in our beautiful lake. It was a hideous green and gray, and it was downright frightening to me. I knew in my heart that it was a monster. Anything that ugly could not be any good. And I hated to see you all lined up on it, looking to me like lambs being led to a slaughter. I should have insisted you find your life jacket. But you kids could hardly wait, and before I could come to my senses and insist, you were on your way.

I believe you were barely ten or eleven years old, Beanie. Well, no one could ever convince Jack that it wasn't his fault. Your mother said she should have insisted you take off the T-shirt you were wearing that day before getting in the water. It was wound so tight around that horrible valve that your little body was pressed up tight against the underside of the tank. We figured you must have fallen forward and when the tank passed over you it somehow caught on your T-shirt.

There you were, our little mermaid, the best swimmer of the bunch, bound up tight to the underside of the beast. And we couldn't get you lose from it, Beanie. It wouldn't let you go.

Poor Jack. He stopped living that day, you know. Packed up and left the cabin and our beautiful lake and our moon and never returned. I tried so hard to get him to come back with me over the years, even if just for a day. But he couldn't do it, Beanie. If I pushed it a bit, his eyes filled with tears and his chin would quiver when he tried to talk. It broke my heart, so I stopped trying. I finally decided to leave him alone. I prayed every day for that man. I prayed he could find a way out of the darkness, out of the prison of guilt he held himself in. He lost so much weight, Beanie. There were times when I thought he would just starve himself to death.

Your momma and daddy tried to help him. They promised they didn't blame him and that they loved him just as much as ever. They begged him to get help. But you know your grandfather. He was a stubborn man, that husband of mine was.

This is awful to say, Beanie, but when he died, I felt a kind of relief. I knew that he would finally find peace and forgiveness. I knew the Lord was waiting for him, to mend his broken heart and ease his troubled soul. I'm happy for Jack now.

You know, we had to cut that T-shirt off of you. It was wound around so tight. We couldn't get it undone, not even loose enough to pull you out of it. And there you were, under that horrible thing, and we were helpless. Your little body, so limp in the water and your long strawberry hair floating out from under that ugly tank. I don't know what we would have done if the Robinsons hadn't been out that day.

Mack Robinson was there, calling for an ambulance, moving Jack and your momma and daddy away from you so he could try and get you untangled. He was an angel sent from God that day, Beanie, keeping his voice steady and quiet and strong. He was so gentle with your little body when he finally cut it loose. And it was Mack that pulled that horrible monster out around the cliffs a few nights later, late at night, and sunk it. Sunk it so none of us would ever have to lay eyes on it again. Sunk it in the deepest part of the lake, down there with the rusted out old cars and the bus. Down there with the rest of the monsters that had claimed lives.

Oh, Beanie. Life took such a turn for the worse after that. It was several years before anyone but myself ventured out to the cabin. It was so abandoned and neglected. You just can't imagine what it was like to open the place up after that. I did it alone. It took days, and I had to ask for some help from the neighbors, but it all got done and the place was as beautiful as ever.

And I felt you there, your presence. I felt your smile and your laughter and your love for all of us and for our little piece of paradise. I knew that if you could, you would have told everyone to celebrate your life and quit mourning your death. Enough is enough. But the others, they don't see things our way, Beanie. I wish they did.

Now they're all upset with me for taking a simple walk that day. Just to revisit my old bridge, just to reconnect with the birds and the willows and the forest, all that I'd been so desperately missing. And finally to find a way for my trouble heart to find peace. I'd spent so many years ministering to Jack, I never had time for my own regrets. It was time.

Angels and Demons

Well, I could hardly drag my old body up into a standing position after I'd had my cry for you. I get so stiff and sore these days, it was all I could do to put myself upright. But your reflection was gone from the water and I felt better, if not a bit drained. I continued on across the bridge, looking at all the little houses lining the channel. They were as pretty as a picture there that day with the sun shining and the leaves falling and all the late summer flowers still in bloom. I heard an eagle cry. It warmed my heart and made me smile.

The rock was just ahead—that huge, smooth, flat stone that soaks up the suns warmth and radiates heat to anyone crossing its path. A warming rock, it is. I stood on the rock on the far side of the bridge and looked back across the marshland and the channel and at all the wildlife. It was warm there, and the heat got my blood to circulate again, I started to come back to life. There were so many birds chirping and swooping—and the willows. Oh! You should have seen the willows that day! I don't know why, Beanie, but they were so majestic.

The breeze captured the long hanging branches and swung them back and forth all together like it was choreographing a dance. I could hear the soft tinkling of the leaves as they snapped together in the process of swinging back and forth, back and forth. It looked to me like they were giant brooms sweeping the marsh clean. In all the years, I've never seen the willows move together like that ever before, and I nearly started to cry. It was such a beautiful sight, and there I was, the only person in the whole world witnessing this wonderful sight, listening to the snap of the leaves as they all moved and changed direction together. It was a beautiful ballet, a waltz being danced just for me, Beanie. A waltz of the willows.

Well, I looked up ahead. I was going to walk down the little dirt road running behind the cabins lining the channel, but when I looked ahead, there was the old logging road, straight up in front of me. I couldn't believe how long it had been since I ventured up that old road. Winter would be coming soon. It was go now or wait until spring. So I decided to be adventurous and walk up a bit. You remember how many times we hiked that logging road all the way over to the other side of the lake, Beanie? So many times any one of us should be able to hike it blindfolded.

Well, it's not much of a road anymore, being all overgrown like it is. I guess folks don't go hiking through the woods like they used to. Anyway, it was calling to me and I answered the call. Just a bit, I told myself. I'll walk a short ways, just a bit up this trail and see what's familiar and what is new.

There were both. My, but the forest has flourished over the years. Every now and then, I would have to push some shrubbery or tree branches out of the way so I could continue up the steady incline of the trail. I had decided that I would turn around as soon as I reached the spot where the trail leveled out. Remember how it climbed for a while and then it leveled out, Beanie? That's all I was doing, just going that far. It was heavenly in that forest, and I was feeling so fine, like a young girl again. So sweet and musky and earthy, all the smells I've missed terribly. I may have even started to forget them, Beanie. How could a person so in love with nature be gone so long that they forget the most important things in life? But the smells were bringing back things forgotten. I was having such a wonderful time remembering all the things I loved about the trees and the mountains and the magic of nature. It was rejuvenating.

What a shame, I told myself, *that I have allowed others to keep me away from what I love.* And for what? What were they trying to save me for anyway—more of these golden years?

I decided it was their problem, not mine, and I wouldn't be held back any longer. I was so proud of the decision I'd made to be there. I planned to journal my way through the seasons and it was exciting to think of getting started, especially after the day's journey up the trail. There would be so much to write about. So, I forged ahead and was enjoying it so much; you have no idea. And I wasn't tired at all, just excited by being reunited with all the familiar old smells and sights and the feeling that one belongs there, in the arms of Mother Nature, in what is real and reliable and true.

There was the biggest squirrel running on up ahead of me and then it just about flew up a tree and began to scold me a mile a minute, for trespassing, I suppose. It's amazing the amount of noise one little squirrel can make. So, I kept going and after a while, I noticed I could no longer hear him. I guess that meant I'd gone a ways, all right.

That little creek—you remember that creek, Beanie? It was trickling water down along the side of the trail for a while before I realized that the creek being there meant I'd gone way past the turnaround point. How did I do that without noticing? I was heading on a gentle downhill slope now, and it was getting hard to see the path. I really thought it was just because of the overgrowth. I didn't realize for a long while that it was dusk. I had decided to turn around and get back out in the open a bit so I could catch sunlight again. I would surely be able to follow the trail better with just a little more light. But when I turned around, there were so many trees and such thick brush in front of me that I wondered just how it was that I'd gotten where I was. I looked all around. Where had the trail gone?

I was having so much trouble seeing in the deep darkness of the thick forest when suddenly I realized what a silly old fool I was. It wasn't dark because I was so deep in the forest. It was dark because it was nightfall!

Well, I took a deep breath and looked carefully around for signs of the trail. I thought I spotted it and headed off in a different direction. I thought it was about right, and it looked like there was a path in there, if I could just get all the overgrowth out of my way. But I was wrong and after a while, I thought it would be best to go back to where I started and get my bearings. I turned to walk back and couldn't tell where I'd come from. That's the moment when it occurred to me that I could actually be lost.

I couldn't think of a nicer place to be lost, yet at the same time, it was kind of frightening. I don't think a soul in the world knew where I was. About then I also noticed how tired I suddenly was and how cold it had become. I was grateful for my wool jacket and my wool socks and for whoever's gloves I had.

Well, I stayed calm and sat down on a fallen down tree. I closed my eyes and inhaled the fresh mountain air and knew I was all right. I thought about walking on a bit farther or trying to head back. I knew I would most likely be able to head back after a rest, as I was very tired out by then. I was feeling the effects of such a long hike on an old body like mine and drained from the emotional journey too and I was thinking it had been quite some time since I'd—and that's when I felt myself slide to the ground, just sink slowly down. I leaned my head against the fallen tree I'd been sitting on and suddenly fell into the most peaceful sleep, Beanie girl, with summer dreams playing in my mind. All sunshine and laughter and children running and jumping off the dock, splashing in the water. All of it coming back to life. It was wonderful. And then suddenly I found myself watching you all climb on to the tank and I was calling for you to get a life jacket on but my voice was silent. I slept fitfully for a while.

I don't know when it was that I first felt the damp cold fingers of an October night creep under my skin and chill my bones. It sent shivers down my spine, an uneasiness that brought me fully awake. I clenched my teeth to stop the chattering, amazed at how much the temperature had dropped. My neck was so sore I could hardly move it, but when I did, I simply lowered myself flat to the ground and snuggled in as close as I could to the fallen tree. It was quite large and offered a bit of protection.

Next thing I saw was the stars; a galaxy of diamonds sparkling and glistening over every inch of an amazing blanket of black velvet sky. I picked them out, my favorites, one by one, and put them on my fingers, diamonds sparkling in the night. The universe was infinitely deep, like there would never be an end to the depth of it. A shooting star streaked across the icy blackness leaving a frosty white trail behind. I was so happy at that moment. Oh, I know I was miserable, so cold and damp and alone. But I was also crazy alive, so much more alive than I'd been in such a long time.

I closed my eyes and shivered from the marrow of my bones through the outer layer of my skin. A breeze was picking up, blowing the branches of the pines like giant arms waving over me. Were they signaling for me to get out or to stay put? I don't know, but they became more and more restless with the oncoming wind. I tried to curl in closer to the tree, pulling my knees up to my chest, but my back was so chilled it felt better to have it flat on the ground. So I looked up again at the stars. There was no moon that night. I don't know where it was, but I sure would have welcomed it. The wind blew stronger, and the trees started to wave their arms every which way, like they were frantic to warn me of something. I would have gotten up and run if I could have, if I had any idea of where to run to. But my body was paralyzed and so snug to the ground, like Mother Earth was holding me firmly in place. I shivered and hugged my arms around me as tightly as I could, pressing myself in as close as possible to the tree and to the ground. I closed my eyes and was surprised to see a glimpse of my angel. I hadn't seen her since I was a child. She threw light and warmth my way for a split second, and I felt hope. I was surprised she'd found me way out there after all these years.

I kept my eyes closed, hoping to catch another glimpse of her, but the wind in the trees was getting stronger and stronger. My eyes opened, and my lovely celestial view was hindered by the frantic whipping of the branches; whipping like they were being thrashed about by the base of their giant trunks. I felt a chill of a different kind—the chill of fear, the chill one gets when evil is present. The skin on the back of my neck prickled. I closed my eyes again and prayed, prayed to my God for protection from the evil I could feel approaching, an evil I was all too familiar with.

Dread crept into my mind and with it a desire to get away. I tried to think of something—anything— good, but couldn't persuade my mind to leave well enough alone. It was the feeling you get when you know you're going to be handed down some bad news and you're trying to prepare yourself and tell yourself everything's going to be all right, even though you know better. That anxiety and dread of something you'll have to explain, of something that'll cost you in more ways than one. That's the feeling I had right then. A very real dread.

I turned on my side and pressed my back into the fallen tree. I held myself as tightly as I could and slowly opened my eyes. I was weak and terrified and alone and all I beheld was blackness. Not a glimpse of light to be found, not even in my heart.

There came a feeling of sinking, as if I'd fallen in quicksand and I was frantically grasping for something to hold on to; anything that would keep me from slipping away; anything that would allow me to continue living. I needed to live for you, Beanie, and for Jack and for myself. Just one more year, I prayed. One more year with my memories; one more year to put all that had happened to rest, one more year to forgive myself.

As a child, my angel would have her wings around me by now, wings of comfort and love. Where was she now that I was old and alone and needed her more than ever before? I screamed out loud, crying for the God who'd forsaken me and for the angel who was my lost guardian. And then suddenly she was there, calming my racing heart. She whispered strength and courage into my ears. She breathed the sweetness of life into my veins. And I opened my eyes wide as I struggled to sit up. The fallen tree offered a branch to grip as I struggled to my feet and held myself straight and tall and came face to face with the demon of guilt and regret. I saw myself watching as Beanie climbed onto the tank that day. I wondered why we saw to it that the others wore life jackets, but not her. We called her our mermaid. We thought she had gills. But I knew better yet I never said anything that day regardless of the nagging anxiety I felt as I watched Jack tow them away. God had given me a warning and I chose to ignore Him.

I knew He had forgiven me and I desperately needed to do the same. I needed to live without the demon pulling me under any longer. I needed to face it and be done with it just as I'd pleaded with Jack to do until it finally destroyed him. I would not allow it to destroy me.

I looked into the red glowing eyes of regret and utter sadness, standing so close I could feel its bitter icy breath and see every detail of contorted pain in the folds of its hideous face. I found strength as I denounced it's hold over me, years and years of suppressed guilt over an accident that should never have happened. Guilt opened its cancerous mouth to scream crippling accusations my way, yet blessed silence was all I could hear. And then claws like scissors tore the demon wide open and all the years of silent torture spilled out until there was nothing left but the peace I so yearned for.

The wings of my angel folded around my exhausted body and lowered me tenderly to the ground and I knew she had never left my side and she never would. I was free. I closed my eyes and once again, I slept.

*R*est

The coldest time of the night is actually in the early morning hours, right around five o'clock. I remember it was black as tar and my body was nearly rattling with shivers when I felt its welcome warmth on my chest.

Do you remember the time the cougar showed up outside the cabin door in the middle of the night? I think you were there that night, Beanie. Remember old Cinnamon? How that dog froze under the bed, so terrified, and Jack had to coax her out with a piece of bacon the next morning?

Well, I'll never forget the cry of that cat, the way it screamed out into the night, blood-curdling cries. I remember Jack whispering in my ear that maybe he shouldn't have been quite so thrifty in his choice of building materials. He was terrified that cat was going to claw its way right on through the walls and tear us apart!

Well, sometime in the early morning hours, when it is absolutely the coldest it's ever going to get, my body started shivering uncontrollably. I was aware of it, yet not, at the same time. I was so cold; every inch of my body ached and my teeth chattered. I remember a shiver running through me that I thought would cause the end of me. It was *so* violent and I was *so* cold. And just about then, when I felt I would probably die of exposure, I had an encounter with the most unlikely creature.

Now, I know this is questionable, but there I was, drifting in and out of sleep, shivering and rattling like the old bag of bones that I am, when the strangest thing happened. I felt warm breath on my face, and whiskers tickled me. I heard the soft humming of a cat's purring as it nudged my face with its own. There was no strength in me to so much as lift an arm and scratch its ear, but the cat didn't seem to mind. It just kept nudging and purring like a little motor.

Next thing I know, there was a heavy fur blanket stretching out on me, right down the length of my body. It was so wonderfully warm and it kept purring as it pushed its face against mine over and over. I know I was supposed to scratch its ears. After all, that's what cats like best, but I was unable to so much as lift a finger. So, I just kept drifting in and out of sleep, enjoying the welcomed warmth and weight of this big ole cat.

I thought about Ollie, Stan, and Willie's cat I'd seen in the rocker on their porch earlier that day. Had it been the same day? It was hard to know, hard to imagine. Well, I wondered if this big ole cat laying on me purring away was Ollie! Could the good Lord have sent Ollie up the old logging road to keep me from freezing to death? Well, anything is possible, but Ollie was just a little house cat. I may have been dreaming, Beanie, but this cat was no house cat. I do believe I was grinning from ear to ear! How many people have a big ole wildcat keep them warm in the bitter cold of the early morning hours? The cat and I slept. Every now and then, I would feel it move just a bit, the purring never ending. And then it was daylight. The cat was gone and the sun was coming up. I was so confused, not knowing for sure if I was dead or alive. I couldn't feel the cold any longer. I felt the earth, and I could smell the richness of the soil. I could hear voices somewhere in the distance, people hollering. It didn't occur to me that it was a strange thing to hear people's voices in a place where I was the only human being. I was so tired. I closed my eyes and drifted in and out for a while. I told myself that I'd be back at the cabin soon, just as soon as my strength returned. I'd light the stove and heat it up nice and toasty and then begin my journal, and oh, what an exciting tale to begin my journal with.

You remember that old log cabin across the road by the community center, Beanie? Did I ever tell you about the little girl that lived there?

Well, I've felt such guilt over that little girl. You know, back in those days, people didn't interfere with the way children were raised. Calling child protective services was unthinkable. In fact, I don't even know if there *was* child protective service back then.

Anyway, for some reason I got to thinking about the little girl living in that old log cabin and the man that was always there with her. I suppose he was her father. I don't know. But he was always so drunk, just falling down drunk, and the girl's mother was never to be seen. I think maybe she went to work every day and the poor little girl was left in his care. How any mother could do that is beyond me. He was a horrible man. I wanted to pick up that child and run off with her every time I saw her. He'd yell at her to get in the house and do this and do that and then he'd holler at anyone walking by. He'd say, "What you looking at?" and, "You got no business here." I often wonder what ever happened to her, Beanie. Whatever happened to that child?

I got thinking about your crazy uncle too. How he had that lady friend living with him with the flaming red hair and those yappy poodle dogs she took everywhere with her. Do you remember how he and your grandpa would go out fishing early on Saturday mornings and catch a bucket full of perch? They'd bring 'em back and clean 'em and then dip them in a batter of flour and salt and pepper. Then they'd fry 'em up in butter and onions and bacon, and we'd eat every last one of 'em. Do you remember how delicious those little fish were, Beanie? That was always the best meal of the week for me: those wonderful little perch with the sweet, tender meat and all the bones I was afraid you kids would choke on.

If I close my eyes, I can still smell the wonderful aroma as it crept up the cabin stairs and into our bedrooms, invading our sleep. Come next summer, I planned to catch some perch and cook them on the grill just the same as we used to do.

For some reason, these were the kinds of things that were passing through my mind that morning; all the while people's voices were calling out in the distance.

And then my thoughts moved on to you and that old tank and the valve your shirt got wrapped around. I thought about what a freak accident that was, and I realized it was probably the first time I'd allowed myself to look at it for what it was, Beanie; an accident.

The voices seemed to be growing louder, coming closer, yet my mind drifted farther and farther away. I couldn't hold myself in the present. I was looking at a tiny snail on the bark of the tree that I was pressed up against. It crept ever so slowly, hardly moving at all, yet leaving a tiny trail behind. My face was so close to the bark of the tree that I could smell everything about it. There is a difference between bark on a tree that is still living and the smell of bark from a fallen tree. It's barely noticeable but it is definitely there, and it caught my attention somehow that day. It brought to mind changes, so many changes we are given no choice but to accept as life moves forward, towing us along.

If the bark had been on a living tree, there would still be the scent of green even if it were an old, old tree. But a fallen tree has richness to the scent, like a wine that has been aged to perfection and speaks of being fully ripe. Not in a bad way you see, but in a regal way. A way that says the massive ropey roots did all they were expected to do. They held up the mighty trunk and anchored it firmly in place for the time allotted by the earth. The bark protected what was vulnerable and grew in thick sticky layers so the tree could climb higher and higher, offering its branches as a resting place for birds, a home to many.

I inhaled the scent of the bark, my nose pressed up against it, and was filled with the realization of a completed existence. My, but how the earth provides in every way. The sense of smell is such a beautiful sense. You know the scent of a newborn baby? That sweet fragrance that only newborns have? I don't even know how to describe it, it's so wonderful. I lay there by the tree, lost in the scent of a baby's tiny head, the soft fuzziness and the intoxicating smell. Just breathing it in made me feel so happy and so warm!

I could still hear voices in the distance but they were farther away now, so far away, but I didn't care. There was nothing as wonderful as the scent I was inhaling all the way down to the bottoms of my feet. Nothing like babies. So soft and warm and pure. Not a trace of the world on 'em in those first few months, just sweetness and innocence and goodness like nothing else God ever made. I felt each one of my children in my arms, laying on my chest, snuggled up under my chin. I inhaled their perfume and lay my cheek on their delicate little heads, gently rubbing my face over the fuzzy little hairs, smiling, happy as I've ever been. I vaguely remember being relieved that the voices were gone. They would surely ruin this perfect memory.

The snail was almost next to my eyes, only inches away. There was a time when the boys and I would walk through the forest after a summer rain for the simple purpose of finding snails such as this one. They came out from under the leaves and pine needles and all their hiding places after a good summer rain.

The shape of their shells was so intriguing. We never stopped wondering of the beauty in the tightly-wound swirl that made up a shell and how the snail itself could completely disappear into its home with barely a trace, fooling us into thinking the house was empty.

Yet there was always evidence of its existence. You see, the snail leaves a tiny trail of slime behind as it goes throughout its life. A nearly invisible trail, but a trail all the same. You can follow the travels of each individual snail by what they leave behind.

I believe each creature, no matter the size, leaves behind something useful to the earth and its inhabitants. I have no idea what the purpose of the snail's slimy little trail is. Maybe it's food for some insects or some such thing. But it was a challenge to see how far a trail could be followed before it was lost in the business of the forest. Not far, I'll admit, but far enough to wonder where it had come from and where it was going.

It's was a very simple example of a legacy. We all leave a trail behind as we wonder our way through the maze of life only to discover in the end how our actions, our attitudes, and our judgments affected those whose path we shared. Who could have known a lesson could be learned from something as simple as a snail.

The snail faded away as did the bark of the tree. Soon, I could only see what was in my mind's eye.

Memories

An old woman's hands floated before me. I couldn't imagine how they managed to be there, as my arms hadn't the strength to hold them up. But there they were; hardy hands with fingers that used to be nimble, fingers that could pick up a penny and pinch a speck of lint off a shirt. My life is etched into the fabric of my hands, from the marrow of my bones to the lines and folds on the surface of my spotty skin. They belong to a woman who worked hard and enjoyed life without the frivolities of some. These hands were not regulars at a fancy nail salon nor did they enjoy the luxury of hired household help. These old hands did it all themselves, creating masterpieces from one day to the next.

They were displayed before my eyes like a painting by God. I pretended they belonged to someone else so I could read them as others would, so I would pay close attention as they signed their story for the world to read.

Old hands they were, yet they shone the beauty of youth behind the layers of age. Anyone could see they belonged to a woman who loved the outdoors. The sunspots and lines spoke of years of too much exposure. They wore short, neat nails, representing a desire for cleanliness and usefulness; ready at a moment's notice, these hands were. And the knuckles were swollen—evidence of days filled with gardening and sewing and writing, all the things a woman does from day to day throughout her life. I closed my eyes and tried to imagine what they would smell like. Maybe cream for a baby's bottom, I decided. Years and years of tending to babies bottoms with tube after tube of creams. These hands were never chapped and dry as long as there was a baby in the house. They were a soft and gentle touch, as always was my heart at the mere thought of my children.

And there was paint, I swear. Tiny specs of paints in all different colors, like a rainbow buried in the pores. They were hands used to create bright, happy spaces in whatever home they lived, hands that baked cookies simply to fill the rooms with the welcoming aromas of melted chocolate chips or warm ginger and cinnamon and raisins, hands that lit cranberry candles at Christmastime and tied ribbons on all the packages under the tree.

There were veins running every which way on the tops of the hands, more obvious than I'd ever noticed before, like the ink from a blue ballpoint pen scribbled in every direction. They seemed to be covered with barely more than the skin of an onion, worn as thin as they were. I was reminded of the worn fabric on the knees of my gardening pants. Hardly any threads left to the fabric and mended so many times, a patch here, a Band-Aid there.

These hands were soft to the touch of a child's forehead as I brushed the hair out of her eyes or held his face as I washed the smear of strawberries off his cherub cheeks. They took care of and nurtured and fixed and held onto and let go of and picked up and put down and received anything and everything a child had to give.

They washed the windows and the children and the dog. They clapped together again and again over years and years of encouraging and praising and congratulating. And they never stopped.

Two of the fingers were decorated with rings, a wedding ring and a mother's ring—a sign to the world that these hands belonged to a woman who has been loved with the passion of a man's heart and with the sweet innocence of a child's. The rings sparkled on the fingers belonging to my own unfailing hands—my faithful, dedicated, never tiring hands. I was grateful and so proud of them at that moment. These lovely, old hands have served me well.

I felt the cold of the morning air once again. My heart was aching. I could feel it aching through my chest. Was the heaviness because it was struggling? Was my heart failing as it struggled to move the blood through my frozen veins? This was possible, I realized, for surely my veins were frozen shut.

Or was it a heart that was breaking into pieces with the realization that I would be leaving soon, leaving all those that I love and hold so close to my heart that there was no longer room for them all? Maybe there is more than one way to die of a broken heart; a heart that is so full of love that it simply hasn't room for any more. Could the weight of all that love finally cause it to tumble down like a stone wall in an earthquake? Big loves and little loves spilling out of my heart every which way, no longer glued together by the ability or the will to take on any more. My heart was full, I realized, filled up and overflowing to the point of breaking, releasing all that love back into the world so it would stay behind—stay and fill up the hearts of those it has held so dear and for such a long time.

I decided that was what was happening to me. All the love was flowing out of my heart and into the hearts of those I would soon leave behind. They would always feel that love and know that I left them with the best gift anyone could possibly have to offer. I only wished to be granted a little more time. Time to pick Mary Millers dahlias and to check on Stan and Willies old cat, Ollie. And time to write this all down for my children and grandchildren.

Once again, I tried to concentrate on voices calling my name in the vague distance, somewhere nearby, but not near enough. I tried to focus on what faces would come into my sight if I could call out. But the faces I saw right then were those of my parents and sketchy fragments of my brothers and sisters. They were all gone from this earth. Wouldn't I be seeing them soon enough? There was no reason to see them yet. I tried to turn away and look at something else, but nothing else would appear before my eyes.

I saw the fog surrounding the valley where we lived and how it laid low far beneath the mountain tops and wound its wispy white fingers around the trunks of hundred year old trees. The silence of the fog was always beautiful to me and it drew me in. It allowed the mind to travel with nothing more in the way than time.

I saw my father's face, lined and tanned, his stern mouth turned down in a permanent frown, his square jaw set firm. His appearance was intimidating. He stood six feet three and two hundred thirty pounds, a powerful figure amongst the farming community of my childhood. Yet if a person dared stand close enough to his mountainous frame and look him in the eye, they would be surprised. My father's eyes were so kind, striking hazel eyes with long, dark lashes and a touch of mischief. They were such a contrast to that famous frown. He could set the temperature at a town meeting just by the look in his eyes. They were the only soft thing about him.

Mother was a beauty with an impossibly thick southern drawl, a permanent smile, and a laugh that sent our happy hearts sailing. She could change the course of history with a flash of that famous smile. But what she did with it was turn the head and the heart of my father whenever his sour mood needed a little sweetening up. She was mighty in her petiteness, and she ruled the roost in ways he never could and in ways he certainly never knew. My mother was a master of femininity.

I saw the stone path leading to the front steps of our two story wood-framed house. Thick green moss and thyme filled in every possible space between the stones. Tiny pink flowers bloomed from somewhere and spread around the ground like confetti.

The roses lining the path were all in bloom, my mother's prize roses. As a child, my favorite was Angel Face because I loved the name. I loved saying my favorite rose was Angel Face, like the name itself proved how special it was and how much I knew about roses.

I climbed the stairs slowly, one at a time, not wanting to miss the familiar creak of the third step. It could be heard inside the house if one was paying attention. I remembered how often I knew someone was coming to the door because of that creaky step. I remembered how often I looked expectantly out the window only to find no one there.

The covered porch wrapped around the whole house and was built of cedar milled from trees on our property. Very few porches are built like this these days; spacious, covered porches with lovely cedar decking and ceilings finished clear to let the natural grain of the wood show through.

I sat down in the swing for a moment and felt the gentle movement as I settle in. Countless hours were spent dreaming in that swing. Dreaming of what my life would be, or where I would go and who I would go with. I smiled at the memory of my youthful dreams, so hopeful and full of adventure. Oh, how much time is whiled away by a young girl with her dreams.

The air was thick. I could almost see the humidity. Yet there was something different in this humidity now. Blinking, I tried to clear my vision, looking for the voices. The clouds parted and sun shone through like on the cover of religious calendars or magazines. God light is what they call it, and it was shining right down on me. How could they miss me with all this God light shining down on me? I was forced to close my eyes to keep from being blinded, and I tried to call out but was struck dumb by the sight before my eyes. There was Jack, standing right in front of me with willow branches draped over his arms. He set them down and then picked them up one at a time, twisting and weaving the tender ends of the branches into intricate wreaths looking like crowns of thorns. But the thorns were nothing more than nubs of new growth with baby leaves attached that became emeralds. They set themselves snuggly in the twisted and braided settings of the wreaths. Then the wreaths became golden, and the brilliant emeralds began to blow away in the breeze, just like the willow leaves they once were. I tried to catch them, to keep them from blowing away but the harder I tried the harder the wind blew taking all the beauty with it. Everything blew away, including my vision of Jack. I wanted to thank him for the gift, for coming to me, but he was gone; gone in the mist and the fog like everything else. Like my parents and siblings were. And our old house with the creaky step.

Simply Being

Is it all a dream? I wondered. Is all of life nothing more than a dream? It seemed that way, so unreal, so untouchable.

Life floated around me, my children and grandchildren all going about their day. No one looked my direction; no one said a word. I tried to talk to them, but they just moved past me, around me, and right through me. Yet I was filled with such a simple peacefulness at that moment, and I knew that they would all carry on without me and suddenly, everything was just as it should be. It was just as any one of us could hope for. I will leave behind a part of myself in their hearts and in some of their mannerisms and like-nesses. I always laugh when I see my granddaughter Emma because she is so much like me. I love to hear the slight waver in her mother's voice when she tells her, "You're so much like your grandmother it scares me." It is said with a hint of pride and a hint of fear. When we leave our families, surely there is a good part of us that they are glad to see go yet an even bet-ter part of us they will miss.

It struck me how odd it was to feel no sadness. I was so content just watching everyone go on. There were friends I hadn't seen in years and people I'd com-pletely forgotten about. They were getting older too, in fact some of them wore an aura of death, yet they were unaware of it. I felt myself so prepared, so ready for the journey ahead. There was no fear or question-ing or regret. I was just ready to go on to the next stage of my life; a different life in a different place. I wondered what my role would be and what my new purpose would be. Under normal circumstances, this would have been exciting, full of adventure and expec-tations. But it wasn't a bit like that; after all, ordinary times were far behind me now. There is only what

God has planned. What a wonderful sense of relief. I just can't explain it, it is heavenly relief.

The ringing in my ears could have been the buzz from a bee, annoying and persistent as it was. I tried to swat it away with my mind as my arms wouldn't rise. It grew louder and louder and then changed from a ringing to the wail of a siren. Wetness embraced my face, at first warm, and then turning cold with the breeze.

I have no concept of time anymore, and I certainly didn't have any the morning I woke on the mountain. I tried to answer the voices calling my name, but my throat was stuck closed and all that came out was a scratchy little croak. I cleared it and tried again and again, but I never did manage a sound. I guessed I would just have to wait until the voices got a bit closer. And they did, in time, with the help of a couple of good scouts.

Next thing I knew, the hounds were barking and nudging their cold wet noses in my face. They were so happy to find me that they made me laugh. At least in my heart I laughed.

Then the voices were right there, pushing the dogs out of the way, asking me more questions than I'd ever been asked in my life. *Good Lord*, I thought, *why such a fuss over an old lady who took a walk and got a little lost?* I didn't want all this attention. But you know, Beanie, I wasn't going to get off easily, now was I?

A man who seemed to be in charge poured water on my face. I think he was trying to give me a drink, but I don't think any of it got to my mouth. He kept pestering me to move parts of my body, and he took my pulse and all kinds of things. I don't know that I actually moved anything or said anything. I was so tired and I couldn't seem to pay attention.

Soon I felt the comfort of nice warm blankets being wrapped tightly around me like you do when you swaddle a baby, and then there was some sort of a stretcher they secured me to. I didn't realize how cold I was until I felt the warmth of those blankets.

Next thing I know, I'm in this hospital room and the whole family is mad at me. They don't know that I can hear them, but I can. If I recover, I will be in maximum security lockdown. Well, I am sorry that I have inconvenienced them once again and I am sorry to disappoint them, but there will be no more restrictions imposed on this old woman.

There is nothing more anyone can do for me here, and I have no desire to live any longer in their imprisoned ways. Too much of life is spent in the scrutiny of the world with eyes upon you that don't really see. How we manage to walk through life, Beanie, with such a heavy veil over our eyes is a mystery to me. Why don't we wake up and remove it so that we can see clearly the ridiculous ways of the world?

I will no longer play in the game of life. It holds no real water, just a sieve pretending to be a reservoir.

There is such peace and contentment in simply being in the place I am in right now. I feel more alive than I have ever been. My senses are acutely aware of everything around me, outside these walls, of the earth, of the universe. Mother Earth is reaching out to me even from deep under the foundation of this building. She is not threatened by the man made world of concrete, steel, and glass. She has the power to shake it to the ground if she chooses.

I am so glad I had a final adventure in my own little paradise even if it didn't last as long as I hoped it would. I am free to go. Free to do as I please, leaving no unfinished business behind. I know they love me, but I also know when a person has worn out their worldly welcome, and I do believe my time has come.

Beanie, please take my hand. I'm ready to come home with you now.

Epilogue

Adeline's children and grandchildren walked together across the bridge. They stopped in the center, twenty-six in all, and looked down into still waters. Their reflections were as clear as a photograph. The only face missing was Adeline's.

They soon continued across the bridge and up the old logging road, eventually ending their journey at the carefully marked spot where Adeline had been found the morning after she spent the night lost on the mountain.

The group gathered around, held hands, and prayed. Her ashes were lifted up to the brilliant sky as the family said a final farewell to the woman whose life had uniquely touched each of their hearts.

A breeze stirred in the trees. It seemed to blow down from the mountain top and whistled through the pine needles as it picked up speed. In a minute it became a wind that whistled hard through the clearing, and Adeline's ashes were caught in a mighty gust swirling high into the sky, released to mother earth, the forest, the meandering creek, and all that she cherished. It was as if Adeline herself flew to the tree tops, swirling and whirling, landing high in the branches, on the petals of wild flowers, and on the sun-drenched forest floor. Her spirit danced around and around, emulating the winsome young girl she once was, until the wind settled and became a gentle breeze again. A quiet stillness gently embraced the clearing. All that was heard were the tears of those she'd loved so tenderly and the soft babbling of the happy little creak.

Good bye, Adeline Leanne McGrath-Cornell— and welcome home.

Endnotes

Adeline Cornell was born in 1911 and died in 1998.

She was eighty-seven years old. The cabin she loved still stands and is cared for by the family. The empty journal has since been filled with stories and memories recorded by her children and grandchildren.

Unfortunately, the road to paradise is still as treacherous as ever.